Affairs of a Cardiovascular Nature

Terry Grimwood

Affairs of a Cardiovascular Nature
by Terry Grimwood
ISBN: 978-1-913766-03-0

Cover Art by David Rix

Publication Date: March 2021

Contents

The Doppelganger's Nemesis

Of course, he's trying to kill me, that figure who lurches out the fog, that featureless silhouette whose face I know so well. I try to run, but it is a heavy-footed stagger through the zigzag streets, a clumsy stumble from shadow-splash to shadow-splash, the animal need for flight, overridden by my nature, the essence of what I am.

I can no more run away than he can end his relentless pursuit.

"Stop" I yell. My voice bounces from the crooked walls, from the twists of crumbling brick, bounced, then smothered by the smoke-stained mist.

"Given up eh Veidt?" the figure shouts back. He sounds as breathless as me.

"You can't do this Veidt," I say.

"Of course I can. I'm your nemesis and a nemesis must nemesise."

"And I'm your doppelganger, and a doppelganger must confront."

"Damn you Veidt!"

A shot rings out and I feel the hot snap of a bullet graze my cheek. I fall back, recover, then spin about and resume my retreat. I force my unwilling body into a shambolic jog. The canted, cobbled road is uneven. Any hazards are obscured by fog. The cold air sears my throat and brings a half-cough, half-sob from my chest.

Another shot, another, loud in the quiet streets, smashing fragments from the walls, scattering shadows that scuttle and slither into the dark between the twisted buildings. This place is bleak but inevitable, more expression than city, formed by, and about, the rotten black kernel of our struggle.

I dart to one side and find myself in a dead-ended alley. There is a wall, against which I fall, clawing for breath now, cheek against the wet cold masonry. The wall is crooked. There is no vertical here, no right-angle or curve.

He appears in the mouth of the alley, a hulking shape, weapon at his side. "Veidt!" I say. "We have to talk. I must show you what you've done. I am what you have done."

"My conscience, is that it? My crime?"

"You killed your wife."

"I was her nemesis. She was a whore. Dear God, I thought I knew lust and passion before I met her; they were nothing compared to … but she trampled my love into the dirt. My love. She mocked me."

"And nobody mocks you, do they Veidt."

"Nobody."

"I was there, I was formed by it. My heartbeat matches the rhythm of those blows you rained down on her skull. Can you hear it? Can you Veidt? My breath is the gurgling of mud-filled lungs. She wasn't dead when you buried her, out there in the night rain, but you knew that didn't you." I gasp for breath, wetly, croaking and sucking at scant air.

"That's why you have to die," Veidt grinds out. "That's why you have to pay." He is walking towards me now, carefully, arm ascending, revolver arcing upwards -

I claw at the wall, find handholds in the rotten brickwork. I wait for the explosion, the white-hot pain. Nothing, only shouted oaths. I twist my head, clinging fly-like. I see Veidt fling the jammed weapon to the ground and leap at the wall.

I wrestle myself onto the narrow summit and kneel, fighting for breath. I peer at the drop on the far side. It dizzies me.

"She had to die." Veidt is hauling himself onto the wall, less than a metre from where I kneel.

"You could have walked away –"

He is up, on his feet, I see a broken brick in his right fist. "No Veidt, I never walk away."

I surge towards him, head low. He grunts in shock as my head slams into his stomach, and staggers backwards. In that last moment, I try to save him, my efforts fruitless and suicidal. His wrist, his hand, slide through mine and he falls. I watch, watch it all, to the last moment.

Oddly desolate, I turn to begin my own treacherous descent.

But, suddenly, I can no longer feel the wall beneath my feet. I am fading, swirling into mist. I have no purpose now, no reason for being. And I realise, as my last thought splinters into shadow and light, that he truly was my nemesis.

Beautiful Are the Feet

How many times have we tried to show you? How many times have you ignored us? You've even had the bad manners to get up and make tea, or worse, go to the bathroom when we try to give you our gospel, our message of hope and light. "How beautiful on the mountains are those who bring good news." The Bible says that and you have the audacity to turn your back on the Bible? Okay, we're being confrontational here, so why don't we all calm down and consider what you're missing, because you're missing life, real life, the real world, the world you, yes that's *you*, can have. We care about you. We care about your skin and your hair and your car and television and internet and your family and friends. And your phone, your mobile device, your *personal* mobile device, your heart, veins, nerves, mind and soul. And no, not the one you have in your hand; nice, yes, useable, but frankly, not much good for much longer, because it doesn't have fUture-gee iConnectivity©, which means that when fUture-gee iConnectivity© comes, and it is coming, you will be isolated, incommunicado, non-communicational. Lonely. No one will be able to talk to you. Not even your own family. *Your own family*, think about it. Speaking of family, you know the old adage, the family that Wii's together, stays together! Fathers are duty-bound to be beaten by their clever-dick kids and made to look like the bungling fools they are. Role models? Come on, so yesterday so *then*, fathers are fun figures, figures of fun. Only single rich men and perfume-splashing androgonoids deserve respect, only back-slapping, seemingly-unattached, thirty-something, white-toothed males on road trips, pub trips and ego-trips are real men. So, play up and play the game, though, well, surely you can't play *War Crime Car Theft Assassin 83* on *that*. Come on admit it. HD? H-Schmee. Flat-screen, okay for some, like your granddad, and the old folks' home. Doesn't come with internet compatibility now, does it? Doesn't have surround-sound, three-dee, hi-viz, eco-trend image-enhancement with integral solar flare dampening, does it? No hope for your soap on that thing. And while we're on that subject, you, and your functional, yes, but somewhat outdated and dull-looking clothes … well, they smell, on a molecular level of course, but an odour is an odour, a foul miasma, a stink. Look at your face, your skin your complexion. Spots, grease-patches, wrinkles. Hag-alert; cream needed, science-appliance, succour from the laboratoire. So, come on, get with the programme between the programmes. Treat yourself, spread a little cash. Spend a little credit, raise a little debt. You want it? Have it. Save? You think you can *save*? Why? Hoarded money is dead money. And, well, isn't it your duty to spend, to oil the wheels. It's your patriotic obligation to the machineries of the nation. All that stuff, all those nice necessities, someone makes them, and you're not willing to support them and their wives and their kids, their cute, clever, shiny-toothed children? What about the fellas who work at the docks, the distributors and shopkeepers and outleteers, you're not willing to shell out a little bit of your money to help them? We're clawing our way out of recession and you want to hoard your lucre and to hide it away as if somehow it will work for you or do you good or buy you things on some rainy day that might never happen. What rainy day? Look at the happy smiling faces we offer, look at the gleaming and glistening and beautiful and tell me that is not real life, the real life you and yours are missing. Are you trying to tell us that you're content to be unconnected, a dirty, frizzy-haired, clog-pored, throwback, a curmudgeon, a retrograde, an anomaly with a vacuum cleaner that doesn't turn corners and a razor that has only fifteen close-shave blades on its flexible head? You're content to be an outcast, a maverick and a fucking individual?

You're content that your children are unbranded, unshepherded, mocked, scorned, bullied, berated, de-rated and hated? Okay, if that's what you want, keep your money, your stash, your cash, and may you choke on it you craven, unpatriotic, luddite, child-hating, self-centred bastard.

Kemistry

"Please, please tell me why I'm here."

"You really don't know?"

"No, I don't. I want my husband."

"He isn't your husband."

"Of course he's my husband. What the hell are you talking about?"

"We don't recognise your so-called marriage to Neil Palmer."

"You don't rec … Look there's a marriage certificate, in our luggage."

"You were already married."

"Divorced. Bloody divorced."

"Not in the eyes of the law."

"I want to call my solicitor."

"Why is that, Judy? Do you think you're under arrest?"

"It feels like it. Your colleagues descended on us the moment we landed at Heathrow, we were handcuffed when my husband protested, our children were taken away … and this looks like a police station interview room –"

"How do you know? Have you been interviewed by the police before?"

"Who are you?"

"How do you know this is a police interview room, Judy?"

"My name is Mrs Palmer."

"Have you been arrested, in the past? Is that how you know?"

"No. I've never been arrested or even been inside a police station."

"Television then, lots of interview rooms on television aren't there: *Frost*, *Lewis*, *Taggart*."

"Who are you? At least I have the right to know your name."

"You haven't actually, but I'll tell you anyway. I'm Dr Anita Rogers. I'm a Police Psychologist. Like *Cracker*."

"Listen, Anita, I am divorced. The decree is in my luggage as well, signed sealed and stamped."

"I suggest you use my correct title, Judy."

"I want my solicitor."

"The law changed after you fled the Country."

"We didn't flee the Country, Neil got a job in Albania."

"What's wrong with jobs in England?"

"Does it matter?"

"Everything matters."

"My divorce doesn't seem to."

"Answer my question."

"Albania is a developing country. They're building out there, hotels mostly and apartments. Neil's an architect. It was a career opportunity."

"Is that all?"

"Yes."

"You're lying."

"What other reason would we have for going there? I mean, Albania for God's sake."

"Why did you come back?"

"Neil's contract has finished."

"Why Albania? Why anywhere? Come on, Judy, tell me."

"I had to get out."

"What? Speak up, for the tape recorder."

"I had to get out."

"Why?"

"You know why. You know everything."

"I want you to tell me."

"God. Look, my ex-husband was threatening me."

"Correction. Your husband."

"Ex, ex, ex, ex fucking ex-husband."

"The law's been changed. You are not divorced from Paul. The marriage stands because it was a chemical marriage."

"A what sort of marriage?"

"Chemical."

"I don't understand?"

"Let me put it this way, Judy –"

"Mrs Palmer."

"Judy. How do you feel about Paul?"

"That's none of your business."

"Yes it is, especially when families are involved. That's my department, Family Maintenance and Reconciliation."

"I've never heard of –"

"It's new."

"New? My God, since when has Family Maintenance and Reconciliation been a police matter?"

"Since the government made it one. Answer my question."

"Okay, okay. I hate him. He's a complete and utter bastard, a fucking bastard."

"You use a lot of strong language Judy."

"Because I've got a lot of strong feelings."

"Hate is a strong feeling, a passionate feeling."

"No, it's just hate. He hurt me."

"But when you first saw him, what about then?"

"I don't have to answer that."

"Yes, you do."

"Christ, this is unbelievable. I fell for him like the sucker I am. Paul was good-looking and tough. He had a six-pack and tattoos and huge biceps and a swagger that turned me on so much it made me wet, okay? Do you want to know more, about the first time we –"

"And what about dating him? Come on, Judy, tell me. How did you feel?"

"Smug. I was Paul's girl, the one he'd chosen me over all the other bimbos who drooled all over him."

"Were you a bimbo?"

"No. I was not. I was set to go to university. I wanted to be a doctor."

"Why didn't you become one?"

"Because of Paul. I was so infatuated I eloped with him. I must have been crazy."

"You were. Crazy in love with the man you desired. Nothing wrong with that."

"Nothing wrong? Of course there was something fucking wrong. It was insanity. I gave up everything for him. I was only eighteen!"

"My point exactly. You love him. That is chemistry."

"Bruises and humiliation, that's what it is … was. He hit me, with those fucking great fists of his."

"Why didn't you run away?"

"I did."

"No, when it started. Why did you stay with him?"

"Because I thought I loved him and we'd get over the bad times and later because I couldn't seem to break away, because I felt as if I had failed and deserved what I got. That's how it is isn't it, with beaten wives? They stay because they can't leave. You're the psychologist, you should know."

"But what was sexual intercourse like with Paul?"

"Go to hell …"

"Tell me Judy and save yourself a lot of trouble."

"What sort of trouble?"

"Just tell me."

"The sex … the sex was good. Always good. But that doesn't mean …"

"Doesn't it? Isn't that what relationships are really about?"

"No, they're not, not completely … I don't know. No."

"You were attracted to him because of his looks, because of his swagger. And the sex was so good you endured physical violence to get it."

"I had no choice."

"Yes, you did, in those days you did. You could've simply walked away. But you didn't."

"I want my children. Where are they? What's happening to them?"

"You could have had children with Paul."

"I love Neil."

"Do you? Really? What sort of love is it?"

"A good love. He cares for me. He's gentle and –"

"Is the sex exciting? Does his swagger make you wet? Does he give you the sort of wild ride Paul gave you? Answer me, Judy; make this easier on yourself."

"No … No, it isn't like that …"

"What is it like?"

"Neil is kind, safe."

"Aha, that word; safe, normal, secure. Boring."

"He isn't boring. God, we've just spent two years in Albania."

"Would you leave him? If another Paul came along? Would you, Judy?"

"Of course not. I love him for God's sake."

"Are you sure? If the chance of another wild ride came? If you met a man who made you wet with his swagger? How safe is your marriage?"

"Very safe."

"I don't believe you. The statistics don't believe you."

"What is going on? I want my husband. I need him. You can't keep me here –"

"Of course we can keep you here. We can keep you here indefinitely. That's how the law works in this country now. There are many threats out there. And what is the worst threat of all? The enemy within, the canker, the cancer, the rot. Family life is breaking down. So many marriages end in divorce. The strongest pillar of our society is crumbling because people leave the ones they are meant to be with, the ones with whom they share that vital chemistry. That's why our enemies despise us. They see us as immoral as dirty, loose, our women flitting from partner to partner, in and out of marriage. They want to destroy us because we are dirty and weak."

"I don't understand …"

"You have to go back to him."

"What … to who? To Neil?"

"To Paul. To your one true love."

"But he hit me. He fucking beat me until I was broken!"

"Because you were hurting him."

"How do you know? What do you know about any of it?"

"He told me. He came to us to claim you back under the law."

"What about my children?"

"Illegitimate, born out of wedlock. Social Services will take care of them."

"I want Neil …"

"He has his own responsibilities; a prostitute he used to see. Became quite fond of her, because she turned him on, because she did the things he really needs, because there was chemistry and he loved her."

"No … No, that's not true. He would never –"

"He was a healthy, normal, lonely man before you met him. And rather naive. It's quite natural, and more common than you think."

"I want to see him."

"I'm sorry. That episode is over."

"God, we should never have come home."

"Not my problem, Judy. You have to face your responsibilities and do what is right."

"And if I refuse?"

"Bigamy carries a prison sentence."

"I'm divorced from Paul."

"You're married to Paul."

"You're wrong … this is insane …"

"No, our society was insane. No self-control, no grit or sense of responsibility. 'Tired of this relationship? Okay, I'll try another, and another, give my virtue to any man who comes along. Ignore what my own body is telling me.'"

"It was telling me Paul was going to kill me."

"It was telling you that you had found what it wanted. We can prove it."

"How? How can you prove something like that?"

"Chemistry. We tested your pheromones, and Paul's –"

"Tested … what are you talking about? You can't test pheromones –"

"– and he's the one, Judy. He's your life partner and the sooner you accept it and agree to go back to him the better. If not … no jury will have an ounce of sympathy, the judge will want to make an example … We have to protect ourselves, and the only way is to repair the walls. Show them, the ones who want to break us, that we are strong and moral and do not deserve their wrath."

"Please …"

"Think about it, Judy. You have time, you're not going anywhere. Think about it, I know you'll do the right, the moral, thing."

"No, listen, you can't go. I can explain, I love Neil. I really love –"

Affairs of a Cardiovascular Nature

"Well hang it all," I exclaimed at breakfast on that frost-hardened, November morning. "She's sent the bally thing back"

"Sir?" inquired my valet as he poured my tea from its silver pot.

"Eleanor's returned my heart. Here." I waved at the just-opened, ribbon-wrapped hat box on the table beside me. "See for yourself."

My valet peered at the black-red organ lying in its nest of ice bags. "It would appear that you are correct sir."

"But, why would she send it back? We're engaged. She said she loved me."

"May I venture to suggest that you read the accompanying correspondence."

"What? Oh, you mean this." I picked up the lilac envelope that had been tucked under the hat box's ribbon. "Jolly good idea."

"My dear dearest darling," wrote Eleanor. "Terrible news! My body is rejecting the heart you gave me as a token of your undying love. How can this be? The doctor swore we were compatible, yet I am betrayed by this vile cage of flesh. I pray you can forgive me, and please, though it will tear your very soul in twain, return my own heart as soon as you can. I have been fitted with one of those clockwork tickers, but it is winding down and tends to leave one breathless. Yours, weeping over our lost love, Eleanor Donnegan-Phipps."

"Puts a bit of a damper on things," I said.

"Indeed sir. Perhaps it would be wise for me to ask 'Shell, our quaintly cockney cook, to place your heart in the new American refrigerating appliance, until Dr Muir can be called to perform the transplant."

"Yes, good thinking." I threw the letter aside. "Better get the deed done this morning. Party at Flapper Boundaby's tonight, I'll need to be on form for that."

"I fear, sir, that you will be forced to send your apologies to Mr Boundaby."

"What?"

"Perhaps this will explain sir."

He handed me a second letter. I recognised the handwriting and Eleanor's heart sank in my chest.

"Dear Nephew," ran this new missive. "Coming to visit, accompanied by Miss Myrtle and one other. Will bring bags for an overnight stay. Your affectionate Aunt, Agatha (Lemon-Amberwick-deWitte)."

"I'll have to put her off," I said, desperate now.

"Unwise sir. You are, as I am sure you remember, a beneficiary in Mrs Lemon-Amberwick-deWitte's will."

"Ah … Yes, didn't think of that. Oh well, I suppose we'd better air the spare rooms and prepare the Hall for battle. You know why the old girl is bringing her Ward Myrtle don't you? She's been trying to hitch us together for years. Dear God, I don't think I can hold out against her in my present state."

"There is one point in your favour sir, something that would render ineffective all Mrs Lemon-Amberwick-deWitte's demands on behalf of Miss Myrtle."

"Eh? What's that then?"

"Well sir, you still possess Miss Donnegan-Phipps' heart. Dr Muir, himself, carried out the transplant and is, therefore, a witness. Should you choose to postpone the return of the organ for one day, the only persons present in the Hall, who know that the engagement is actually broken, are yourself and I. Therefore, as far as Mrs Lemon-Amberwick-deWitte and Miss Myrtle are concerned, Miss Donnegan-Phipps still possesses your heart, and you sir, still possess hers, which renders you officially betrothed."

"Mmmm ... right, I think I understand old chap. Wizard thinking ... I'm sure. And Eleanor can jolly well wait for her heart. It'll serve her right ... that is what you meant isn't it? That I keep her heart for an extra day?"

"Yes sir."

"Thought so. Well, time to man the battlements and –"

"You will, of course, have to inform Mrs Lemon-Amberwick-deWitte of your alleged engagement to Miss Donnegan-Phipps. I fear sir, that she may be somewhat displeased."

"Yes, yes you're absolutely right. No other way is there? I mean, you couldn't do it for me could you?"

"It would hardly be appropriate sir."

No, I realised as I watched Aunt Agatha's gleaming battleship of a car crunch majestically up the gravel drive after lunch, it would not be appropriate. Oh well, nothing for it but to stiffen the old upper lip and take it on the chin like a ... well, a man I suppose.

A chauffeur opened the door smartly and Aggie emerged, flags a-flutter and guns primed for a broadside. Myrtle followed, a skinny specimen with a permanently sniffly nose, horsey teeth and a shock of bright red hair, mostly concealed under a rather fetching cloche hat. Her ankle-length, tight-fitting coat made her look like a giant, fur-trimmed worm.

Forcing a smile onto my face I strode down the stone steps to greet my visitors. As I brushed my lips over the back of Aggie's glove-clad hand, I spotted the third member of her party. A tall, cadaverous fellow with skin as pale as death and an expression less animated than that on my late father's face as he lay in his bed awaiting the arrival of the undertaker.

"Church," Aggie explained in low tones. "My bodyguard."

"Bodyguard?"

"Ssssh you nincompoop. You'll frighten poor Myrtle, she thinks he's my doctor. I need a bodyguard on account of Smiling Sam Copechne."

"But that finished years ago." Oh God, my Aunt's one wild fling, her sole whirlwind romance, had been with some overweight charmer she met while holidaying in America just after the war. His name was Samuel Copechne and he turned out to be a gangster, and a bootlegger to … well, to boot. It had taken all my valet's wisdom and wit to extract the old girl from that one.

"Years ago or not, he didn't take it well when I turned down his offer of marriage. And he is known to bear a grudge."

"Surely you're quite safe here in England."

"The arm of vengeance is long," she whispered dramatically then swept into the Hall, leaving me with a blushing, simpering Myrtle, and Dracula's younger brother.

Gathering my courage, I kissed Myrtle's hand, which sent so much blood to her face I thought it would explode, rather messily, over my new tweeds.

Church followed, not shaking my hand, or even looking at me. Simply walked past, freezing the air into spiralling wisps of fog in his wake. Something distinctly odd there.

Afternoon tea, dominated by Aggie and heavy with lingering glances and shy smiles from dear old Myrtle, was followed by the inevitable inspection of the gardens. What's so exciting about soil and plants, that's what I want to know? But Aggie always insists, so out we went, bundled in coats, scarves and galoshes. It was foggy, dank and utterly miserable. Didn't deter old Aggie, though, nothing deterred her.

Church brought up the rear, freezing the mist as he walked by, and turning the puddles to ice.

We found Umbrage the gardener in the vegetable patch.

"What a wonderful crop of Brussels my good man," Aggie declared.

"Ahhhrr." muttered Umbrage.

"So green, so lush!"

"Ahhhrrr," Umbrage agreed solemnly.

"What's the secret?" Aggie said, with a rakish, conspiratorial air.

"Ahhhrrr," confided Umbrage, in a loud whisper.

Dinner was a tiresome inevitability, especially as I knew that just five miles down the road, Flapper Bounderby's party was getting under way without me. Myrtle, wearing a nice dress I must say, was on top form. She simpered and grinned and stared and gasped and tittered at my every word.

"Must be lonely in this big old house," Aggie declared over dessert. "What do you think Myrtle?"

"Yeth Mitthus Lemon-Amberwick-deWitte."

"Could do with a woman's touch eh?"

"Yeth Mitthus Lemon-Amberwick-deWitte." This time accompanied by a giggle and a bright red face.

"Well actually," I muttered, seeing my moment, no doubt the way a Tommy would have seen his moment just before going over the top. "It may have that woman's touch sooner than you think."

Myrtle looked as if she was about to faint and Aggie positively beamed. Suddenly I felt rather low; poor Myrtle, decent sort really, didn't deserve a broken heart. Still, best to put a lame horse out of its misery.

"I … Uh … Um … you see … well …"

"Oh, do get on with it man," Aggie barked.

"Yeth … I mean yes, of course. You see …"

"My master is currently engaged, madam, to Miss Eleanor Donnegan-Phipps." Oh bless you my faithful valet.

"Donn … The *Bedfordshire* Donnegan-Phipps?"

"The very ones madam."

"Good gracious. They're tradespeople I believe, new money. How ghastly."

"Aren't you happy for me aunt?" I tapped my chest. "She's given me her heart you know."

"Happy? *Happy?*"

At that moment, poor Myrtle erupted into hysterical tears and fled from the table. On the way she knocked over a wine glass, which shattered and spilled broken glass and a nice, rather pert French red onto my lap. I fumbled at the glass and cut myself. So now there was blood all over the place as well.

Quick as a flash, Church grabbed my hand. I flinched, waiting for him to sink his teeth into the wound - but no, he snatched a handkerchief from his top pocket and gently wiped away the blood. Then my valet was there, flourishing a napkin with which to wrap the injury. The bodyguard retreated, the red-stained handkerchief clenched in his ashen fist.

And that wasn't the end of the night's festivities, by a long straw. Oh no …

Something woke me, deep in the long watches. There was a scream and a gabble of voices.

I scrambled out of bed and bounded along the passage to the stairs, pulling on a dressing gown as I went. Dashed cold I can tell you, but I couldn't very well stay in bed when women were screaming could I?

When I reached the landing, I saw Aunt Aggie and a clutch of servants standing over a figure who appeared to be lying on the floor. As I hurried downstairs I saw that it was Church.

Blood trickled from a small hole in his chest and pooled from what was obviously a much bigger one in his back.

"Thank goodness poor Myrtle was asleep," Aggie said breathlessly as we sipped brandy in the drawing-room later.

"Yes, I suppose there is that about it. But look, we should phone the police."

"Good gracious me no," she snapped. "All those awkward questions. What if the newspapers got hold of it? Reporters everywhere, prying into my private business. No, I know who killed Church. It was Sam."

"Copechne? Here?"

"Well, not exactly. The murderer was a slim, shadowy type, wearing a hat low to hide his face and a mackintosh with the collar turned up. But I'm sure he was sent to do the deed by Sam. He must have thought poor Church was my ... well, gentleman friend."

My valet entered, he wore a heavy coat and carried a torch. "I am afraid my search for the culprit has proved fruitless sir," he said. "I have, however, taken the liberty of organising the staff to search the grounds."

"Top hole. Don't know what I'd do without you old chap."

"I have also dealt with the remains of the unfortunate Mr Church madam."

I suspected that there would be an even finer crop of Brussels sprouts next year.

Aggie and Myrtle left the next morning. I must say that poor old Myrtle looked a little white and weak. Not surprising, I suppose. Had her love spurned and a travelling companion murdered, all in one night.

Actually, white and weak is something of an understatement. She looked, to coin a phrase, like death warmed up. She could barely walk and clung to Aggie's arm like a survivor clinging to a piece of wreckage. Taking it all a bit too hard in my opinion, after all, it's wasn't my fault I was engaged to someone else … well, actually, I wasn't. But I might have been. Hang it all, I felt a complete rotter as I watched her shuffle down the steps towards the car.

However, just before she got into Aggie's shiny black dreadnought, the oddest thing happened. Myrtle glanced over her shoulder to give me a dazzling smile and mimed kiss. I was quite stunned. I'd never taken young Myrtle for a flirty type, but she was downright vampish at that moment. I have to say that I found it rather, well, stimulating.

Guests gone, I retired to my room to await the arrival of the good Dr Muir, and the return of my own heart.

The anaesthetic wore off late in the afternoon. I woke, feeling rather queer, all sweaty and shivery. My heart fluttered and stumbled in my chest. I rolled over, stretched for the bell-rope, overreached and fell out of bed. I hit the floor with a thump, knocking the air out of my lungs and the stuffing out of my resolve. I hauled myself towards the door, sure I was dying and in need of my valet.

I was almost there when it opened to admit Dr Muir.

"Good God mon!" he gasped. "Up, pull yeself together. Put some steel into your spine. Och, you're no but a Sassenach sissy."

"Would if I could old chap," I gasped, "But I'm feeling jolly unwell."

"Unwell? No one feels unwell at the hands of Doc Muir."

Annoyed at being judged a sissy, I tried to stand, but halfway up the steel in my spine gave way. Back on the floor, I sweated and blew like a landed trout. Dr Muir frowned. "Does seem tae be some sort of problem here laddie. Best get back into bed."

"If I didna ken better," he muttered as he tucked me in. "I'd say you're rejecting your own heart, but it's nae possible, nae possible at all."

"No disrespect now doc," I ventured breathlessly. "But could you have accidentally popped someone' else's ticker into the old cavity?"

"What?" he roared, face reddening, jowls a-tremble. "How dare ye!"

"Sorry. Silly idea."

But Dr Muir was mortally offended and stormed from the room before I could apologise properly.

Then it dawned on me. Eleanor had sent the wrong heart back to me. Accidentally of course. One that belonged to some other rejected beau perhaps. I needed my valet. Time was running out. A chap can't live long with the wrong heart.

So out I climbed again, more carefully this time, and staggered about until I bumped into the door and lurched out into the passage. I made it to the stairs and as I tumbled down to the hall, noticed that the bloodstain was gone. There was, in fact, no sign that a grisly crime had ever been committed in my house at all. Filled with affection for my splendid and always trustworthy manservant, I lurched into the passage leading to the servant quarters.

"Sir?" my valet said as he opened his door to me. "Are you quite well?"

"No, I'm not quite well. In fact, I feel rather dickey if you must know. Look old chap may I sit in your room?"

A flicker of something crossed his features. I was startled. His features were not the habit of flickering. "Of course, sir."

My valet's quarters were rather bare, just the bed, a chair, a small table, a wardrobe and … well, that's all. No photographs of loved ones, no pictures on the wall, no trinkets or mementoes, nothing but those four pieces of furniture. Yet, that emptiness was somehow a richer and more extravagant portrait of its owner than the most crowded study could ever be.

"Dr Muir's given me the wrong heart," I gasped as I huddled on the edge of his bed. "I don't know how it happened, but it did. Any thoughts on the matter old chap?"

"I was in attendance during the entire operation sir. It was I who fetched your heart."

"Well dash it all, someone must have swapped it."

"That is a possibility sir, but the only other persons with access to the refrigerating appliance are myself and 'Shell, our quaintly cockney cook."

"I say, you don't think the old girl thought it was a sheep's heart and served it up to us last night do you?"

"Hardly sir." My valet offered a small, but hugely reassuring smile. "The container was clearly marked."

"That's a relief."

"You do realise," I continued. "That if I don't get my old heart back, or one that's compatible, I'll be dead by dinner."

"The possibility had occurred to me sir."

"Well get your thinking hat on. I'm too young to pop me clogs."

I closed my eyes and was surprised to see Myrtle, looking over her shoulder and smiling that oddly vampish smile. She was very pale. I had assumed that it was because she was distraught at losing so fine a catch as me. But …

… Myrtle's paleness was deathlike, dark rings under her eyes.

"Oh my God!" I exclaimed.

"Sir?"

"Myrtle! Myrtle has my heart, and I have … hers?"

"But who?"

"That bodyguard chappie they brought with them. Perhaps he really was a doctor. I've been duped, deceived and murdered. Call the police! Call Scotland Yard –"

"Is that wise? An unfortunate event took place last night sir, one we have, as they say, covered up. Awkward questions may be asked. One's reputation might suffer."

"But one's life is about to end –"

"Indeed. But, perhaps we should approach this on a diplomatic level sir."

"Dip … There isn't time." With that I collapsed back onto the bed, my strength waning.

"I have taken the liberty, sir, of sending a telegram to the young lady concerned, my suspicion having already been aroused." He consulted his pocket watch then returned it to his striped waistcoat. "She will be here at any moment sir. I would advise rest."

When I awoke the light outside had changed from gold to black. My borrowed heart banged away like some old jalopy with its cylinders all awry.

A moment later my valet entered. He carried a silver plate upon which was a letter. Paper rustled, he cleared his throat, then read; "Dear nephew. Myrtle is feeling rather poorly. Her heart is broken, her soul bereft, all hope dashed on the rocks of your cruelty. Also, I lost a perfectly good gentleman friend due to your carelessness. You will not be hearing from me again. Yours etc Agatha etc. PS: When I depart this mortal coil, do not trouble yourself to attend the reading of my will, it will be a wasted journey."

"What are we going to do?" I wailed.

"Fear not sir, I have taken the liberty of ordering your car and driver. It will, however, be a somewhat difficult journey for you."

"No matter! There comes a time in a chap's life when sacrifices need to be made. We must drive through the night as if the very Devil is at our backs!"

And what a journey. It was a rattling clanking bump and judder along endless roads and moonlit lanes as my life ebbed away. Until, at last, we reached London, where, after negotiating the incomprehensible maze of the capital's streets, we attained Grosvenor Gardens and parked outside Aunt Agatha's humble abode.

My valet went to the door, carrying a few items of medical equipment as he did so, to save time. He was met by Aggie's butler, disappeared inside, and after an absolute eternity, emerged again.

"I have explained your predicament, sir, and managed to persuade the good lady to allow you entrance."

"Has a doctor been called?" I managed to croak.

"No need, laddie," said the chauffeur, throwing off his peaked cap. "I'm sae sorry I shooted at you earlier. So, I'm here to make it up to ye. I'll perform the operations and put things right in a jiffy!"

"Well bless me!"

"I took the liberty of recruiting his assistance in this venture. I trust it was in accordance with your designs sir."

I could have kissed my valet at that moment, but, well, refrained … chaps, you understand, not done.

The bedroom had already been prepared. There was no sign of Aggie, or of her small staff. She had, so my valet explained, no wish to see me. Bit harsh, that, considering my proximity to death's door.

And there was poor Myrtle, a pale stain on the sheets, wan, corpselike. Something tumbled over inside me.

I was helped me onto the bed beside her and lay back gratefully. "Sorry old thing," I whispered. She stirred and muttered something. I hoped it was forgiveness.

Dr Muir busily attached a rubber hose to the gas bottle my valet had carried inside when we had arrived. He fitted a mask to the other end of the hose then approached the bed.

Myrtle's eyes opened wide and she uttered a cry.

"No! Pleathe … all wrong …"

"Och, there now lassie. Dinna be frighted. A'will be well, a'will be well."

"Blood …" she gasped.

"Aye there'll be blood, but it'll be cleaned up afore ye wake. Now breathe deep."

He lowered the mask towards her *pretty* little face.

Feebly she tried to push it away then screamed "Blood … Blood tetht …"

"Blood test?" I asked. "What blood test?"

"Church … Doctor … Compatible …"

I forced myself up onto my elbows, about to tell her the truth about Church, when I remembered the broken glass, the blood, his handkerchief, the way he'd popped it into his pocket once my valet stepped into the breach, and the coldness that surrounded him. What if he was not a bodyguard but a doctor all along, one of those haematology chappies who make a fat living testing to see if couples are compatible before they go swapping hearts and getting hitched.

"What're ye saying lassie?" Muir asked.

"I fear she is delirious doctor," my valet said.

"Seems you've got my heart after all," I said to Myrtle. "But poor old Churchy was wrong about us being compatible." Then a penny dropped and I propped myself up to stare at my valet. "Wait a minute. You're the only person who knew where my heart actually was last night."

"Yes sir. I must confess that I was a willing participant in Mrs Lemon-Amberwick-deWitte's plot."

"Aunt Agatha? But why didn't you tell me?"

"I felt sir, that you would not be amenable to such an arrangement, but I also believed that Miss Myrtle and yourself were meant for each other."

"Hang it all, old chap, you can't go swapping hearts around willy-nilly –"

"You're right," said a cool, familiar, female voice. "It would have been much simpler just to shoot you."

The entire universe slipped sideways, because Eleanor Donnegan-Phipps was the speaker. My Eleanor, gorgeous in fur coat and delicate veiled hat. In one hand she held a cigarette holder, in the other, a pistol. And it was pointed at me.

"Oh, do get out of the way and give me a clear shot, darling," she snapped and for a moment I thought she was talking to me, but then I realised that she was actually speaking to my valet and the universe finally flipped onto its back and I was hanging on for dear life.

"Your impatience is understandable," my valet said. "But I believed that any hint of murder would have been detected by the gentlemen of Scotland Yard. Instead, there would be a set of untimely deaths brought about by an unsuitable swapping of hearts. And, of course, a grieving valet who did everything in his power to save his master after trying to bring two star-crossed lovers together. Regrettably, however, I am forced to defer to your cruder methods, my dear, and include Dr Muir in the tally of victims. I had anticipated that Miss Myrtle would be deceased, and therefore silent, by the time we arrived. And that my master – my *erstwhile* master – too dim-witted –"

"I say, steady on."

"– to untangle the web of deceit I had so carefully constructed, before he too succumbed."

"Aunt!" I shouted, panic giving me enough strength to yell out to the old girl. "Aunt Agatha! Help!"

"A futile gesture sir. I took the liberty of giving Mrs Lemon-Amberwick-deWitte and her staff a hearty whiff of Dr Muir's gas when I entered the house upon our arrival." My valet shook his head sadly. "Now, Eleanor my dear, perhaps you would shoot these people. In the case of my master, please be so good as to put the bullet in his head."

"My head? Damned gruesome, not like you at all. At least have the decency to go for my ... Hang on ... You wouldn't be attached in some way to the ticker beating away in my chest would you now?"

"Indeed, I am sir."

"Good Lord," Muir exclaimed. "Ye mean, I put *your* heart in ..."

"Yes Doctor."

"And *his* heart was already in ..."

"Yes Doctor."

"My God," snarled Eleanor. "Why the hell do you want *his* heart?"

"Because my devotion to my master is perhaps a little deeper than appropriate. I saw this as an opportunity to express, in a small and secret way, the full extent of my affection. I was fully aware, however, that the attachment ran only in one direction, and such a demonstration, therefore, would prove fatal."

"Well hang it all old chap. I … We … I …"

"And what of your affection to me?" Eleanor demanded of my valet, her lover, in a dangerously shrill voice. "Why did you marry me?"

Marry her? "Marry her?" I exclaimed. "What … When … Why …"

"Her fortune, of course. Now safely signed over to me in her will. And there was the sex, Eleanor my dear, my appetites are somewhat catholic."

"So, whose heart have I got if I haven't got yours?" Eleanor demanded.

"Miss Myrtle's."

"*What?*"

"And, once again, madam, it would appear that there is some deeper and unreturned affection on your part, seeing as you are perfectly healthy, but Miss Myrtle is gravely ill."

"Are you suggesting …"

"I rather think he is old thing," I said. "So how did you get Church to do all this swapping about?"

"Dr Church, sir, was a back-street haematologist, struck-off for acquiring a taste for his patient's blood. Not wanting his secret revealed to the authorities, he was most co-operative. The procedure was somewhat complicated. First, he removed my heart, placed it in the refrigerator and inserted yours into my chest. Then he anaesthetised and operated upon the two ladies, in separate rooms of course. Eleanor had, by the way, entered the Hall disguised as a member of the domestic staff. Both Mrs Lemon-Amberiwck-deWitte and Miss Myrtle were convinced, of course, that the other patient was yourself sir. Instead, Miss Myrtle now possesses Eleanor's clockwork heart. Sadly, the mechanism is running down."

"So where is my heart?" Eleanor demanded. "Seeing as it isn't in your chest."

"Once Dr Muir had removed it from my master this afternoon, I took charge of the organ, claiming that I would package and send it to you. Instead I planted it beneath the Hall's vegetable garden."

"Beside poor old Church no doubt," I said. "And who better to blame for his demise than Smiling Sam Copechne. Or was it frowning Eleanor Donnegan-Phipps in yet another disguise? You seem very comfortable with that gun Eleanor."

"Hah!" she sneered.

"The game's up Eleanor," I said, my voice no more than a whisper. "Your lover doesn't love you and you don't love who you think you love and the person you don't realise you love certainly doesn't love you."

"Never!" Eleanor laughed maniacally, raised the gun until I was staring down its little black barrel, and fired.

Chaos broke loose. Then the smoke began to clear and I realised that the body sprawled across the floor wasn't me. And there was Aunt Agatha, poker in hand, hair all dishevelled but looking rather magnificent. Eleanor was, staggering about, holding her right arm and shrieking out the most awful curses.

I saw the gun, lying on the floor.

Eleanor saw it too.

I was off the bed in a trice, crawling across the floor until the old arms and legs gave way. On my belly now, I groped for the weapon. A spiked heel drove into my hand and I yelped. Panicking, I grabbed at Eleanor's fine, stocking-clad leg with my good hand. Down she came, right on top of me. We lay there for a moment, all entwined and panting, her face inches from mine. I forgot myself. And so, I think, did she, because our lips got pretty close before I jerked back. Eleanor cursed and gave me the sort of clout round the head that would've made my late father proud. Then she wriggled away, going for that gun again.

I clutched her ankle and she kicked and bucked and screamed. But I held on, though the light was fading and all I could hear was my faltering heartbeat.

Held on … until Dr Muir swept by and snatched up the gun and it was all over.

*

"Aunt Agatha," I gasped after Eleanor was securely tied up and gagged beside my slightly wounded ex-valet and I'd been helped back onto the bed. "I thought you were gassed."

"I was, but I was never fully under."

"A small error laddie," said Dr Muir. "You see, a lonely old man like me needs a little entertainment of a cold evening, so I like to take a wee sniff of gas now and then, a weak mixture mind, which is what was in the bottle your valet mistakenly brought indoors."

"Stroke of luck that old chap. Anyway, we haven't time for idle chit-chat. Myrtle needs her heart back."

"Aye laddie, and so do ye. I'll fetch the real gas from the car and put that fur-wearing hussy under, then get on wi' the job."

"No," I said. "Knock my valet out so you can dig *my* ticker out first eh?"

"Good gracious!" Aggie cried out. "You selfish bounder. I always knew you would come to no good –"

"Aunt, please. I want Dr Muir to give my heart to Myrtle, and I'll have hers. They are compatible I believe."

Did He Fall,
or Was He Pushed?

So, what have we got? Let me get this straight. There was you and this broad. What was her name again? Jill, right? Jill. Okay, so what happens, refresh my memory here. You got a surname by the way? Huh? Everyone's got a surname. Okay, keep your stupid mouth shut, it don't bother me. So, we got you and Jill. What are you, brother and sister, lovers, man and wife? Come on, you might as well open up. Help me, I help you. No? Ah, suit yourself. Anyway, you two set off up the hill, to get some water. Water? What the fuck you doing going *up* a hill to fetch water? Water don't stay on top of hills, it runs down the sides, everyone knows that. Anyhow, you're going after this alleged water, when you fall. She push you Jack? Huh? Let's say she did. Let's be hypothetical. Why would she push you? Insurance maybe? Good old insurance, they oughtta have a health warning on life insurance. Okay, maybe not insurance. You two have a fight up there? You try to rape her? You drunk, or is it drugs? Makes sense don't it, the two of you stoned outta your fucking heads. Maybe you thought you was flying up that hill, maybe that's why you thought the water was sitting on top of the hill, or maybe, now listen up, this is good, this is what I call a theory, maybe, water's a code word for narcotics. Yeah, think about it. You two go up the hill to where you've stashed the coke cola and you get greedy and start fighting just like those guys in that Humphrey Bogart movie, you know, "The Gold of the Sierra Whatever", and down you come. Hey, hey, wait a minute, Jill comes down too. "Tumbling after," that's what you told Officer O'Grady. She lose her footing? You pull her down with you? So, what happens at the bottom? Christ, it says here you had a fractured skull. Some fall. Not only that, you walk away. Fractured skull my ass. You get a fractured skull Jack, you ain't gonna be walking away from nowhere. Hey, hey, you're not even walking, you're running, as fast you can, "caper" you call it. Caper, yeah, that's a good word, because the whole thing sounds like a caper to me. So, what you do next, Jack the marathon caperer with a broken crown? You go to the Emergency Room? Nah, you do what any good citizen of this Country would do, you try fixing your own head. And you know what Dr Jill uses? Huh? Vinegar. Vinegar! What the hell use is vinegar? And brown paper. Why brown paper? Why not white paper or green paper? No, brown paper. Vinegar and brown paper. You gotta be stoned mister. But let's forget all that bullshit for a moment. What I wanna know is this, what happened to Jill. We've found no sign of no Jill. Last time you mention her, she was tumbling. She exist Jack? She real? Or, maybe you've buried her somewhere …

War War

"Excuse me."

"Yes?"

"Are you …?"

"Yes, if you're …"

"I am."

"Jolly pleased to meet you, old chap. Sit down. I hope this table is all right. It's my usual."

"It is perfect."

"Discreet enough?"

"Yes."

"Sorry, I haven't done this sort of thing before. Not sure of the etiquette."

"Were you not briefed?"

"Oh, yes, I was briefed, but nothing can quite prepare you for the real thing, can it."

"I suppose not. But, you don't seem very sure of yourself."

"Please, let me assure you, I have received a thorough preparation."

"Very well. How much authority have you been given?"

"Absolute. I represent government, business and the military – Ah, the menu, thank you. Drink?"

"Vodka."

"G and T for me. I've already settled on the Dover sole. Always excellent here. But take your time, old chap. No rush."

"Steak, rare. I want to see blood on my plate. Now, leave us, please."

"Impatience? Not a good quality for this type of discussion is it."

"My superiors are impatient. I haven't time to ponder menus. We should begin with timescales."

"Well, you see, that's a little difficult."

"In that way?"

"You're going to think us rather foolish."

"Unless we know when to commence, we can make no further progress. This is a complete waste of time –"

"Please, please, sit down, there's a good fellow."

"Very well. Give me your suggested date."

"January the first."

"Are you insane? In the middle of winter? *Our* winter?

"We have our reasons."

"Suicide is not a good reason."

"Bear with me, old chap. A mistake made by many an army has been to attack you in the spring. Perhaps they didn't understand just how vast your country is, or perhaps they underestimated your resilience. Whichever is the case they all ran out of time and were decimated by that winter you're so proud of. *Start* in the winter and by spring you will be halfway to your objective."

"But the *winter*?"

"Come now. You know as well as I do that times have changed; clothing technology, all-weather aircraft, cruise missiles. A shortage of anti-freeze for our tank engines isn't going to pose much of a problem these days."

"Even so …"

"It's our preferred option."

"And you are certain of this."

"Certain."

"If you fail, it will end too quickly and benefit no one."

"We don't believe either side will be able to make any decisive victories in the winter."

"I do not believe that winter is a sensible solution."

"Surely your armed forces are sufficiently equipped to operate during winter in your own country."

"Of course they are."

"Then what's the problem? It isn't as if you and I will be out there freezing our balls off, is it."

"Public opinion –"

"A little ironic coming from you."

"We are a democracy –"

"Really? And how long has your president been in power? How many elections won against fierce opposition?"

"Sarcasm is unhelpful. And what of your so-called democracy? Most of your politicians come from private schools. Your class system is as undemocratic as you believe our own to be. A system rigged against the proletariat."

"Surely you don't undervalue a good education"

"A good education, open to all."

"Oh dear. That old nonsense again. You're beginning to sound like one of those tired old men watching the rockets being driven by on May Day."

"You don't believe in equality? Opportunities for everyone, no matter their background?"

"There are limits, old chap. You can't expect some oik from a sink estate to leave their comprehensive school prepared for the intricacies of international politics now, can you."

"Sink estate?"

"You know what I'm talking about. Ah, the food. The sole looks exquisite. Steak bloody enough for you?"

"Perhaps. So, if we agreed that hostilities commence in winter, who starts it?"

"You."

"Why us?"

"It'll be far more convincing … What's so funny? I fail to see the joke."

"Us? The aggressor? Given your recent record?"

"We needed the oil and Halliburton needed the contracts. Come on, you know as well as I do that it doesn't matter who starts it. A spot of global conflict is good for the economy. A chance to reduce unemployment, and to stir up a bit of patriotism, everyone pulling together, sing-songs in the air raid shelters."

"All right. Suppose we agree to make the first move. What reason could we give? What have we to gain? How much money do we have invested in your country, eh? How much property, how much finance propping up your banks? And what about the black economy?"

"I hardly think drug money –"

"The world's economy is one big money laundry and you know it. Your assumed naiveté is wearing thin. *You* attack *us* or the deal is off."

"Off? I don't think that's possible. The train is running down the track dear fellow, can't be stopped."

"We have provoked you. We have pushed you. We have interfered and invaded and even committed murder on your own soil. We have muddied the waters in the Middle East. We have backed the worst leaders and governments in the world. And still you hold back. Still you show no spine. What more can we do?"

"All right, all right. You've given us the motive. We need an opportunity."

"We are both playing in the sand. Our toys are lethal. An accident is inevitable; another downed airliner, a cruise ship torpedoed. The possibilities are endless."

"Mmmm, I see your point. Very well, we'll start it if you agree to a winter kick-off."

"I think I can persuade my people of its merits. A toast."

"Cheers."

"We must be careful not to end it too quickly."

"Oh, I think the winter will bog us both down long enough for attrition to kick-in. Stalemate. Trenches even. Back to the good old days eh? Millions of shells being blasted across No Man's Land. Just one fly in the ointment though. Two actually."

"Flies?"

"China, and North Korea."

"What about them?"

"Well, won't they want to join in? I know North Korea will want to side with you lot, but China? Not so sure."

"They'll stay out of it. They'll be looking to sell us all cheap armaments."

"Quite, but we can't have them undercutting our own manufacturing base. Our countries have mutual arms contracts in the offing. Delicate negotiations underway. Can't have China elbowing in. I think we should get rid of them early on."

"Get rid of China?"

"Yes."

"How do you suggest we get rid of a country?"

"Well, there's the blunt instrument."

"Suicide, mutually-assured."

"All right. What about some of the stuff we have locked away at Porton Down? And I'm sure you can find some canisters of nastiness lying around somewhere."

"Imprecise."

"There will be some overspill, true. The wind might blow some germs one way or the other but, in the scheme, of things, that isn't such a problem. It'll look like collateral damage."

"It is not possible to destroy an entire nation."

"But we can hamstring them for a while. Some of our stuff is pretty lethal and quick. They won't have time to react or retaliate."

"Interesting idea. I will consider it."

"Now, it's time we dealt with the elephant in the room."

"Not to be used until we are in stalemate, then tactical only."

"Yes. Might work in our favour. There'll be panic. A rush to the negotiating table."

"Negotiating … No, no, the last thing we want is an early end to this –"

"Of course we don't, but a ceasefire would give us all a bit of a breather, time to regroup."

"What about escalation?"

"Escalation?"

"It would seem unconvincing if tactical strikes did not become strategic ones."

"Yes. It would. Got it! A brutal conventional air raid, on a capital, one that doesn't matter, enough dead and burned women and children to rouse the public anger, thirst for revenge. It would lead to a tit-for-tat, a handful of cities on either side.

"Unimportant ones, of course."

"Of course."

"Wouldn't want to damage our industrial base."

"Absolutely not."

"I am growing to like you, my friend."

"You're not so bad yourself, old chap. So, what have we got so far? Slow war. Bogged down by winter and supply shortages, which will give us all time to dig in for the summer, perhaps a costly assault by ourselves in August or September. A heroic failure always goes down well. Desperate bravery, posthumous medals."

"We will need our turn as well."

"How about a heroic rear-guard action in the following spring, as you retreat."

"Retreat?"

"The public won't countenance an endless stalemate. There has to be some drama to pique their interest. A Dunkirk moment, perhaps. Then we toss some tacticals at each other and move on to a strategic or two."

"A bold plan. I think my people will be satisfied."

"You know, I think a few nuked cities will be the perfect way to bring this thing to a thundering climax. Just the thing for an emotional plea from all sides about the waste of human life blah blah blah."

"Peace is declared, followed by joint reconstruction projects between our nations. Wounds healed. A global world order. But we will need a new enemy eventually, something with which to frighten the masses into acquiescence and keep production levels high."

"Oh, I think we can go back to playing in the sand once our little spat is over. Plenty of factions and revolutions to stir up. Nothing better than a little proxy war now and then to raise the temperature, eh?"

"A toast to playing in the sand."

"I'll second that. We have a saying back home."

"Yes?"

"Paraphrased a bit, you understand, but it goes like this: where's there's rubble, there's brass."